STAND UP SPEAK OUT

ANIMAL RIGHTS

Virginia Loh-Hagan

GO VEGAN

STOP POACHING

BE kind to every kind

1

45th Parallel Press

Published in the United States of America by Cherry Lake Publishing Group
Ann Arbor, Michigan
www.cherrylakepublishing.com

Reading Adviser: Beth Walker Gambro, MS, Ed., Reading Consultant, Yorkville, IL
Book Designer: Jen Wahi

Photo Credits: © Andrea Domeniconi/Shutterstock.com, 4; © novak.elcic/Shutterstock.com, 6; © Jakub Stepien/
Shutterstock.com, 8; © ARTFULLY PHOTOGRAPHER/Shutterstock.com, 11; © everydayplus/Shutterstock.com, 12; © dezy/
Shutterstock.com, 14; © patarapong saraboon/Shutterstock.com, 17; © Rawpixel.com/Shutterstock.com, 18; © EQRoy/
Shutterstock.com, 20; © MOLPIX/Shutterstock.com, 23; © khlungcenter/Shutterstock.com, 24; © Jason Cassidy/
Shutterstock.com, 26; © Nico Faramaz/Shutterstock.com, 29; © timsimages.uk/Shutterstock.com, 30, additional cover
images courtesy of iStock.com

45th Parallel Press is an imprint of Cherry Lake Publishing Group.

Library of Congress Cataloging-in-Publication Data

Names: Loh-Hagan, Virginia, author.
Title: Animal rights / by Virginia Loh-Hagan.
Description: Ann Arbor, Michigan : Cherry Lake Publishing, 2021. | Series:
   Stand up, speak out | Includes index and bibliographical references.
Identifiers: LCCN 2021004985 (print) | LCCN 2021004986 (ebook) | ISBN
   9781534187504 (hardcover) | ISBN 9781534188907 (paperback) | ISBN
   9781534190306 (pdf) | ISBN 9781534191709 (ebook)
Subjects: LCSH: Animal rights–Juvenile literature.
Classification: LCC HV4708 .L64 2021 (print) | LCC HV4708 (ebook) | DDC
   179/.3–dc23
LC record available at https://lccn.loc.gov/2021004985
LC ebook record available at https://lccn.loc.gov/2021004986

Printed in the United States of America
Corporate Graphics

About the Author:

Dr. Virginia Loh-Hagan is an author, university professor, and former classroom teacher. She's currently the Director of the Asian Pacific Islander Desi American Resource Center at San Diego State University. She is a fan of animals, especially dogs! She lives in San Diego with her very tall husband and very naughty dogs.

TABLE OF CONTENTS

Activists often work as a group. They have power in numbers.

WHAT IS ANIMAL RIGHTS ACTIVISM?

Everyone has the power to make our world a better place. A person just has to act. **Activists** fight for change. They fight for their beliefs. They see unfair things. They want to correct wrongs. They want **justice**. Justice is upholding what is right. Activists help others. They serve people and communities.

Activists care very deeply about their **causes**. Causes are principles, aims, or movements. They give rise to activism.

Many activists feel strongly about animal rights. They don't view animals as property. If humans have rights, then animals have rights too. They're living beings. They deserve the best life possible.

Animal rights activists make people aware of animal

suffering. They support being **vegetarian** or **vegan**. Vegetarians don't eat animals. Vegans don't eat or use animal products. This includes eggs and cheese.

Animal rights activists want to stop the use of animals by humans. They want to stop animal **cruelty**. Cruelty means harm and abuse.

In this book, we share examples of animal rights issues and actions. We also share tips for how to engage. Your activist journey starts here!

● Animal rights activists work with environmental activists. They protect animals' homes in the wild.

GET STARTED

Community service is about helping others. It's about creating a kinder world. Activism goes beyond service. It's about making a fairer and more just world. It involves acting and fighting for change. Choose to be an activist!

○ **Focus on your cause!** In addition to the topics covered in this book, many other causes help animals. These include saving endangered animals, banning trophy hunting, and improving factory farming.

○ **Do your research!** Learn all you can about the cause. Learn about the history. Learn from other activists.

○ **Make a plan!** Get organized.

○ **Make it happen!** Act! There are many ways to act. Activists write letters. They write petitions. They protest. They march in the streets. They perform art to make people aware. They post to social media. They fight to change laws. They organize sit-in events. They participate in demonstrations and strikes. During strikes, people protest by refusing to do something, such as work.

Ancient Greeks were among the first to write about animal testing.

CHAPTER 1

STOP ANIMAL TESTING

People use animals for research. They catch animals from the wild. They also **breed** animals for testing. Breed means to mate in order to produce young. Scientists test drugs on animals. Companies test products on animals. More than 100 million animals are used around the world every year.

The **Humane** Society of the United States is a group of animal rights activists. Humane means kind. This group hosts a global "Be Cruelty-Free" **campaign**. Campaigns are organized courses of actions. The campaign's goal is to end **cosmetic** testing of makeup and other personal care products on animals. Group members write letters to companies. They ask people to buy cruelty-free products.

Lush is a cosmetics company. All Lush products are 100 percent cruelty-free. Lush supports laws against

GET INSPIRED

BY PIONEERS IN ANIMAL RIGHTS ACTIVISM!

○ **Lizzy Lind** was a Swedish anti-vivisection activist. Vivisection is the cutting of living animals while they're awake. She gave speeches. She founded a group to fight vivisection.

○ **Coles Phinizy** was a journalist. He wrote an article for *Sports Illustrated* in 1965. It was about a Dalmatian dog named Pepper. Pepper was stolen by dognappers. She was used for animal testing and died. Phinizy's article brought awareness to the issue. It inspired the Animal Welfare Act (AWA) of 1966. AWA is a U.S. federal law. It sets standards for animal treatment and care.

○ **Dr. Jane Goodall** created a new way to study chimpanzees. She got close to chimps in the wild. Her work changed how people thought about chimps. She worked to improve the lives of chimps in zoos and labs.

animal testing. They organized a "Fighting Animal Testing" campaign. In 2012, they hosted a performance artist in a shop window. The artist underwent some of the tests that are performed on animals, such as force-feeding. The point was to show how much animals suffered during the tests. That same year, Lush started a cash award for people doing work to end animal testing. Since the award's launch, there have been over 110 winners from 28 countries.

Animals also sometimes stand in for humans. Scientists wanted to send people to space. But first, they tested on

Animal rights activists support buying and wearing cruelty-free products and clothing. These products are not made from animals.

animals. Laika was a Russian dog. In 1957, she became the first animal to circle the Earth in a spacecraft. She died soon after launch. Activists in Great Britain hosted a minute of silence. Another group attached signs to their pets. They marched outside the United Nations building in New York.

Stand Up, Speak Out

Many things in your house may have been tested on animals. These products may include cleaners, candy, tissues, and tape. Companies test products to make sure they are safe for humans. Activists think animals need to be safe as well. They want to end animal testing. You can help!

> Don't buy any products from companies that test on animals. Read labels. Do research on the companies. **Boycott** these companies. Boycott means to avoid or not buy something as a protest. Write letters telling the companies why you won't use their products.

> Buy products from cruelty-free companies. Support these companies to encourage them to make more cruelty-free products. Post good reviews of them online.

Pit bulls are the most common dogs used in dogfighting.

CHAPTER 2

END ANIMAL FIGHTING

Animal rights activists don't like using animals for entertainment. Animals are used in circuses, TV shows, and movies. They're used in racing events. They're also used in blood sports. These fighting events are the most harmful. The most common fighting animals are dogs and **cocks**. Cocks are roosters. People abuse animals and raise them to be violent. They force animals to fight to the death. They bet money on the fights.

Rebecca Corry is an actress and comedian. She has a pit bull named Angel. She started Stand Up for Pits in Los Angeles. She hosts a tip line. People can report dogfighting events. Corry hopes to catch animal abusers. She also wants to rescue abused dogs.

GET INSPIRED

BY LEGAL VICTORIES

○ Jennifer Graham became famous for saving frogs. In 1987, she was a student at Victor Valley High in Victorville, California. Her teacher assigned her to dissect a frog. Dissect means to cut up in order to study. Graham refused. The school threatened to fail her. Graham sued the school. She fought in the courts for 4 years. In 1998, California supported Graham. The state passed a law letting students choose alternatives to dissection. Other states adopted this law. This law is known as "Students' Rights Options."

○ For many years, dogs and cats were raised as food animals in China. Today, animal rights activists in China fight to ban the eating of dogs and cats. They work with politicians. They host education campaigns. They stage protests. In 2020, the southern Chinese cities of Shenzhen and Zhuhai banned eating pets. They became the first Chinese cities to do so. Government officials began calling dogs "companion animals."

Many activists fight against cockfighting. They've sued the people and places hosting these fights. But in some cases, cockfighting is part of the culture. For example, it's a tradition in the Philippines. This makes it hard to stop.

In Spain, bullfighting is popular. Some people think it's a tradition or even an art form. But animal rights activists think it's animal cruelty. In 2019, activists staged a

● Cockfighting was popular in ancient India, China, Persia, and Greece.

demonstration. They were only wearing underwear. They wore horns. They taped outlines of bulls on the street. They lay down in the outlines like bodies in a crime scene. They had signs reading, "Stop bullfighting."

Chickens are actually very friendly.

Stand Up, Speak Out

Dogfighting is **illegal** in the United States. Illegal means against the law. But people still do it. They host dogfighting events in secret. They do this to make money. Activists want to stop dogfighting. You can help!

> Host a march. April 8 is National Dogfighting Awareness Day (NDFAD). Make signs. Walk your dogs.

> Sign a petition to support the Help Extract Animals from Red Tape (HEART) Act. Rescued dogs can't be adopted until the court cases prosecuting dogfights are settled. The HEART Act wants to speed up the court process. It makes the criminals pay for the costs of caring for the dogs.

Activists are also critical of national zoos and petting zoos.

CHAPTER 3

BOYCOTT ROADSIDE ZOOS

Some people buy or **poach** wild animals. Poach is to steal. People take animals from their natural homes. They cage these animals. They set up roadside zoos. They abuse the animals or don't provide proper care.

Caged animals get bored, stressed, and lonely. Many captive animals get an illness called **zoochosis**. Animals with this disease rock and pace. They may even hurt themselves.

Animal rights activists are against these zoos. They don't think animals should be used to make money or entertain humans. Wild animals should be able to roam free. Humans shouldn't breed, capture, or cage animals.

GET IN THE KNOW

KNOW THE HISTORY

○ 1635 The first known animal rights law was created in Ireland. The law was called an "act against plowing by the tail and pulling the wool off living sheep." First, it protected horses. At this time, farmers tied a horse's tail to the plows. This hurt the horses. Second, the law protected sheep. It banned pulling wool off live sheep.

○ 1866 The American Society for the Prevention of Cruelty to Animals (ASPCA) was formed. It's the first animal rights group in the Americas. Henry Bergh founded the ASPCA. Bergh stopped a carriage driver from beating his fallen horse. This action inspired him to help animals.

○ 1931 Mahatma Gandhi was an Indian activist. In London, he argued for vegetarianism as a way to protect animals.

○ 1944 Donald Watson was an English animal rights activist. He invented the term "vegan." He formed the British Vegan Society.

The Association of Zoos and Aquariums creates standards of care for zoos to follow. Many zoos follow these guidelines.

Tony the Truck Stop Tiger was an animal at a Louisiana roadside zoo. For more than 7 years, Animal Legal Defense Fund activists worked to free Tony. They fought for a big cat ban. They wanted to move Tony to a **sanctuary**. A sanctuary is a place of safety. Animal sanctuaries do not buy, sell, or breed animals. They take care of unwanted or injured animals. Tony got sick in 2017. He had to be put to death.

Joe Exotic is known as the "Tiger King." He owned a zoo in Oklahoma. He bought and bred big cats.

He killed 5 tigers. He illegally sold wild animals. He tried to have Carole Baskin killed. Baskin is the founder of the Big Cat Rescue Sanctuary. She hosted protests against Joe Exotic. Joe Exotic is now in jail.

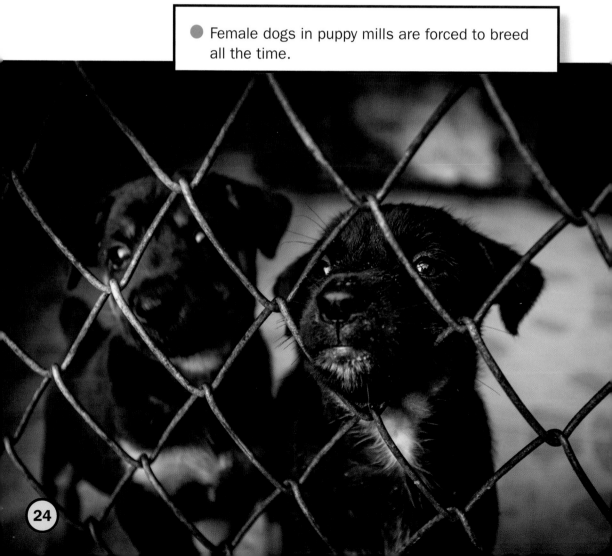

Female dogs in puppy mills are forced to breed all the time.

Stand Up, Speak Out

Learn more about puppy mills or puppy farms. These places breed and sell puppies. Many activists don't like the puppy mills. Puppies and their parents are held in cages. They're often abused or neglected. Activists want to put puppy mills out of business. You can help!

> Write letters to your local politicians. Ask the city to shut down these stores.

> Boycott stores that sell puppies from these mills. Tell your friends not to buy from these stores.

> Encourage people to adopt from animal **shelters**. Shelters take care of animals that don't have homes. Make posters showing why it's better to adopt than to buy pets.

Whales are Earth's largest animals. Many migrate from the tropics to the poles.

CHAPTER 4

SAVE THE WHALES

Whaling is the hunting of whales. The whales are killed for human use. People eat whale meat. They feed meat to their pets. They make carvings from whale bones. They use whale **blubber** to make oil. Blubber is fat.

Whaling creates problems. Whales almost became **extinct**. Extinct means to no longer exist anywhere. Whales are needed to keep oceans healthy. They help the environment.

Anti-whaling activists think whaling is inhumane and not needed. "Save the Whales" is a very successful campaign. It started in the 1970s. Activists wanted to increase awareness. They made badges and pins. Many people wore them. This campaign inspired change.

GET INVOLVED

There are several groups working to protect animal rights. Connect with them to get more involved.

○ **GAP** is the Great Ape Project. Its members believe apes have the rights to life and freedom. They fight against taking apes out of the wild.

○ **PETA** is People for the Ethical Treatment of Animals. Ethical means honest and kind. PETA is an animal rights group. They believe "animals are not ours to experiment on, eat, wear, use for entertainment, or abuse in any other way."

○ **SPCA** is the Society for the Prevention of Cruelty to Animals. They want to stop animals from getting hurt. They rescue abused and unwanted animals. They take care of animals and find them new homes.

○ **FARM** is the Farm Animal Rights Movement. They fight for farm animals. They promote a vegan lifestyle. They host a national conference. They promote compassionate holidays. These are holiday meals without meat.

The International Whaling **Commission** is a group of more than 80 countries. Members of the group study and protect whales. They banned whaling in 1982. This saved the lives of many whales. But 3 countries still kill whales. The countries are Japan, Iceland, and Norway.

Whale-watching makes more money than whaling.

Greenpeace and Sea Shepherd are anti-whaling activist groups. They interfere with the whale hunting season. For example, they go to oceans near Japan. They look for Japanese whaling ships. The activists go out in small, fast boats. They get between the whaling ships and whales. This way, whalers won't attack whales for fear of attacking the activists.

● Whales and dolphins live in groups. In captivity, they're taken away from their families.

Stand Up, Speak Out

Killer whales and dolphins are **marine** mammals. Marine refers to the sea. These animals don't do well in captivity. They don't live as long as those in the ocean. They don't have enough room to swim freely. They get skin problems. Activists want killer whales and dolphins to be in oceans. They don't want them in tanks. You can help!

> Find an **aquatic** park near you. Aquatic is having to do with water. Find out if the park has captive marine mammals. Ask if it forces them to perform. Find out if it breeds the captive animals. If so, write the park a letter. Ask the park's leaders to stop.

> Learn more about sea sanctuaries. Create a social media campaign to support the sanctuaries.

GLOSSARY

activists (AK-tih-vists) people who fight for political or social change

aquatic (uh-KWAT-ik) having to do with water

blubber (BLUH-bur) fat

boycott (BOI-kot) to refuse to buy something or take part in something as a protest to force change

breed (BREED) to mate in order to produce young

campaign (kam-PAYN) an organized course of action

causes (KAWZ-es) the reasons for activism

cocks (KAHKS) roosters or male chickens

commission (kuh-MIH-shuhn) a group with a specific goal

cosmetic (koz-MET-iks) having to do with makeup or beauty products

cruelty (KROOL-tee) the inflicting of pain or suffering

extinct (ek-STINGKT) to no longer exist

humane (hyoo-MAYN) kind and compassionate

illegal (i-LEE-guhl) against the law

justice (JUHSS-tiss) the upholding of what is fair and right

marine (muh-REEN) of the sea

poach (POHCH) to illegally steal

sanctuary (SANGK-choo-er-ee) a place of safety and refuge

shelters (SHELL-turs) a place that takes care of unwanted or abused animals in the hopes of finding them permanent homes

strikes (STRYKES) organized protests where people refuse to do something

vegan (VEE-guhn) a person who doesn't eat or use any products derived from animals

vegetarian (vej-uh-TER-ee-uhn) a person who doesn't eat animals

whaling (WAY-ling) the hunting and killing of whales for human use

zoochosis (ZOO-choh-siss) a sickness of captive animals resulting in swaying, pacing, rocking, and self-harming

LEARN MORE!

Loh-Hagan, Virginia. *Temple Grandin and Livestock Management*. Ann Arbor, MI: Cherry Lake Publishing, 2018.

Marsico, Katie. *The Humane Society*. Ann Arbor, MI: Cherry Lake Publishing, 2017.

Woods, Bob. *Animal Testing: Attacking a Controversial Problem*. Broomall, PA: Mason Crest Publishers, 2018.

INDEX